PRO SPORTS SUPERSTARS

SUPERSTARS OF THE NEW YORK GIANTS

by M.K. Osborne

AMICUS | AMICUS INK

Amicus High Interest and Amicus Ink are imprints of Amicus
P.O. Box 1329, Mankato, MN 56002
www.amicuspublishing.us

Library of Congress Cataloging-in-Publication Data
Names: Osborne, M. K., author.
Title: Superstars of the New York Giants / by M.K. Osborne.
Description: Mankato, MN : Amicus, 2019. |
Series: Pro sports superstars NFL | Includes index. | Audience: K to grade 3.
Identifiers: LCCN 2017057976 (print) | LCCN 2017059318 (ebook) | ISBN 9781681514918 (pdf) | ISBN 9781681514093 (library binding) | ISBN 9781681523293 (pbk.)
Subjects: LCSH: New York Giants (Football team)--Biography--Juvenile literature. | New York Giants (Football team)--History--Juvenile literature. | Football players--United States--Biography--Juvenile literature.
Classification: LCC GV956.N4 (ebook) | LCC GV956.N4 O74 2019 (print) | DDC 796.332/64097471--dc23 LC record available at https://lccn.loc.gov/2017057976

Photo Credits: All photos from Associated Press

Series designer: Veronica Scott
Book designer: Peggie Carley
Photo researcher: Holly Young

Printed in China
HC 10 9 8 7 6 5 4 3 2 1
PB 10 9 8 7 6 5 4 3 2 1

TABLE OF CONTENTS

Get to Know the Giants 4
Emlen Tunnell 7
Frank Gifford 8
Lawrence Taylor 11
Michael Strahan. 12
Eli Manning 15
Jason Pierre-Paul 17
Odell Beckham Jr. 18
Young Star 21

Team Fast Facts 22
Words to Know 23
Learn More 24
Index 24

GET TO KNOW THE GIANTS

The New York Giants joined the **NFL** in 1925. They have been to five Super Bowls. They won four of them.

Who are some of the Giants' greatest stars? Let's find out!

45

EMLEN TUNNELL

Emlen Tunnell was good at **intercepting** passes. He was part of the "Umbrella **Defense**" in the 1950s. They made great defensive plays for the Giants. Tunnell was the first African American to be elected to the NFL Hall of Fame.

FRANK GIFFORD

Frank Gifford was good at everything. He was a fast runner. He could catch. He could pass. He even kicked. Gifford played in the **Pro Bowl** at three different positions.

Gifford was the Giants' first draft pick in 1952.

GIANTS
56
MC MAHO
9

LAWRENCE TAYLOR

Lawrence Taylor changed how **linebackers** played. He was fast and strong. He was good at tackling. He was the second player picked in the 1981 NFL draft. Taylor was the NFL **MVP** in 1986.

MICHAEL STRAHAN

Michael Strahan has more **sacks** than any other Giants player. He set a record in 2001. He helped the Giants win a Super Bowl in 2007. He played in seven Pro Bowls.

Strahan (#92) was voted into the NFL Hall of Fame in 2014.

ny
10
Wilson

ELI MANNING

Eli Manning is a quarterback. He shines the most in big games. He led the Giants to two Super Bowls, in 2007 and 2011. He was named Super Bowl MVP for both games.

JASON PIERRE-PAUL

Jason Pierre-Paul plays defense. The Giants picked him in the first round of the draft in 2010. He helped them win a Super Bowl in 2011. He has been to two Pro Bowls.

ODELL BECKHAM JR.

Odell Beckham Jr. joined the Giants in 2014. He had a great **rookie** season as a wide receiver. It was the best in NFL history. He had 12 touchdowns and 91 catches for 1,305 yards. He has been to three Pro Bowls.

Beckham Jr. is known for doing silly dances to celebrate when his team scores.

YOUNG STAR

Sterling Shepard is a wide receiver. The Giants drafted him in 2016. That year he caught 65 passes for 683 yards. He can jump high to catch the ball.

Let's watch and see who will be the next star of the Giants!

TEAM FAST FACTS

Founded: 1925

Home Stadium: MetLife Stadium
(East Rutherford, New Jersey)

Super Bowl Titles: 4
(1986, 1990, 2007 and 2011)

Nicknames: The G-Men and Big Blue

Hall of Fame Players: 19
including Emlen Tunnell, Frank Gifford, Lawrence Taylor, and Michael Strahan

WORDS TO KNOW

defense – the group of players that tries to stop the other team from scoring

intercept – when a defensive player catches a pass

linebacker – a defensive player

MVP – Most Valuable Player; an honor given to the best player each season

NFL – National Football League; the league pro football players play in

Pro Bowl – the NFL's all-star game

rookie – a player in his first season

sack – a tackle of the quarterback on a passing play

LEARN MORE

Books

Burgess, Zach. *Meet the New York Giants.* Chicago: Norwood House Press, 2017.

Mack, Larry. *The New York Giants Story.* Minneapolis: Bellwether Media, Inc., 2017.

Websites

New York Giants—Official Site
http://www.giants.com
Watch video clips and view photos of the New York Giants.

NFL.com
http://nfl.com
Check out pictures and your favorite football players' stats.

NFL Rush
http://www.nflrush.com
Play games and learn how to be a part of NFL PLAY 60.

INDEX

Beckham Jr., Odell, 18
Gifford, Frank, 8
Manning, Eli, 15
MVP, 11, 15
NFL, 4, 7, 11, 13
Pierre-Paul, Jason, 17
Pro Bowl, 8, 12, 17
Shepard, Sterling, 21
Strahan, Michael, 12
Super Bowl, 4, 12, 15, 17, 18
Taylor, Lawrence, 11
Tunnell, Emlen, 7